This Next New Year

JANET S. WONG · PICTURES BY YANGSOOK CHOI

Originally published by
Frances Foster Books · Farrar, Straus and Giroux · New York

pomelo ✳ books

YUZU
an imprint of Pomelo Books

www.janetwong.com
www.yangsookchoi.com
www.pomelobooks.com

Current edition published by Yuzu, an imprint of Pomelo Books.
Originally published by Frances Foster Books / Farrar, Straus & Giroux
Text copyright © 2000 by Janet S. Wong
Illustration copyright © 2000 by Yangsook Choi

Library of Congress Cataloging-in-Publication Data is available.
ISBN 978-1-937057-25-1

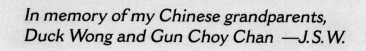

In memory of my Chinese grandparents,
Duck Wong and Gun Choy Chan —J.S.W.

To my grandmother, Kang Yonglae —Y.C.

This next new year
is about to begin,

not the regular new year,
January 1,

when we watch the Rose Parade
and football games

and make crazy
New Year's resolutions,

but the lunar new year,
the day of the first new moon.

I call it Chinese New Year
even though I am half Korean

and my mother cooks *duk gook*,
the Korean new year soup.

My best friend Glenn, who is French and German,
calls it Chinese New Year, too,

even though he celebrates it at his house
by eating Thai food to go.

And my other best friend Evelyn,
who is part Hopi and part Mexican,

says Chinese New Year
is her favorite holiday

because she likes to get red envelopes stuffed with money
from her neighbor who came from Singapore.

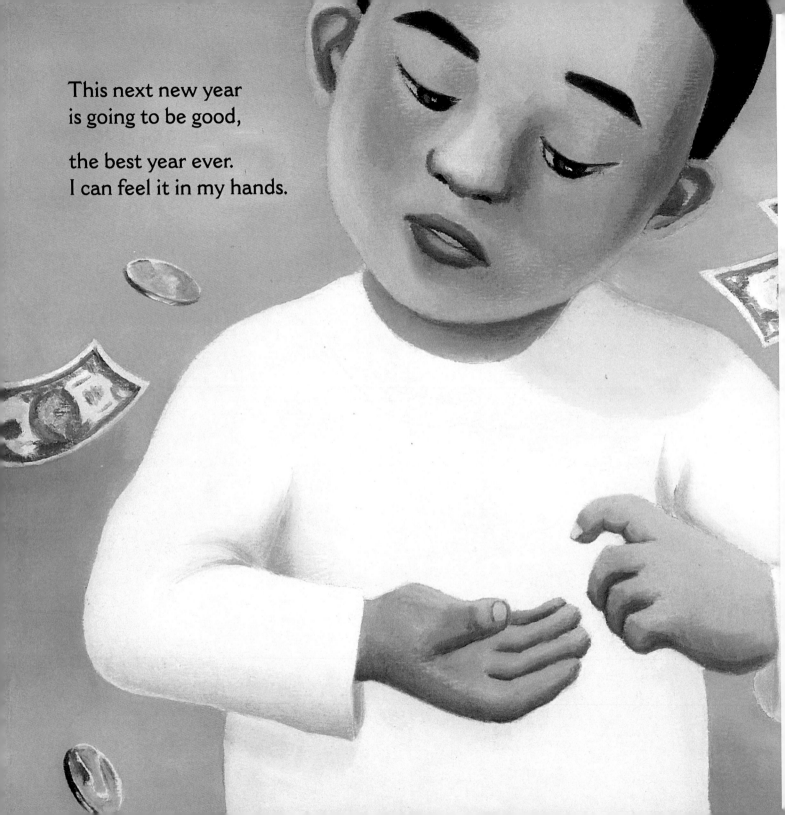

This next new year
is going to be good,

the best year ever.
I can feel it in my hands.

They say you are coming into money
when your palms itch,

and my palms have been itching
for days.

My brother thinks it's warts,
but I know the luck is coming

because we've started early, for once,
and our luck is long overdue.

Mother is sweeping last year's dust
into piles so big

all I can figure is
no wonder we've had so much trouble lately.

I will move these mountains of bad luck off the floor and into the trash,

brushing every last crummy crumb into my dustpan.

One last piece of the porcelain vase
that broke when the ball

slipped out of my hand—
        gone!

A river of leaves from the plant
that died even though I meant

to water it soon—
        gone!

The cricket I found one day in my shoe
who made a good pet

until he escaped—
Oh, poor cricket, I looked for you—

all that bad luck,
            gone!

We are scrubbing our house
rough and raw

so it can soak up good luck
like an empty sponge.

And tonight I am washing my hair
and drying it extra dry

so it can soak up some good luck, too,
and that luck can drip into my brain

and come to my rescue
at school.

I am cutting my nails
and even cleaning the dirt out from the corners

of my big toenails
so the luck can squeeze itself in there

and take me
where I want to go.

I am flossing my teeth
so I will have something smart to say

next time
you catch me by surprise.

I don't have the new clothes I need
but I have saved the cleanest ones I own

for this big day
and if everything works

you can bet
I will have new clothes soon.

This year I am not going to jump out of my skin
when we light the firecrackers at midnight

to scare the bad luck away
and wake up all the neighbors.

I will be brave.

I will not even hide my face
inside the crowd during the parade

when they light the long strings of firecrackers
that pop pop pop pop pop pop pop

all over the place.

And all day tomorrow,
Lunar New Year's Day,

I will not say one awful thing,
none of that

      can't do
      don't have
      why me

because this is it, a fresh start,
my second chance,

and I have so many dreams,
so many dreams

I'm ready
now

to make
come true.

Author's Note

The lunar new year is made up of twelve months. Each month begins on the day of the new moon and has twenty-nine and one-half days. A lunar year is normally only 354 days long except during a leap year, every three years or so, when the Chinese lunar year is made longer by a "leap month." But I never knew any of this when I was a child. I never wondered why the lunar new year happens at a different time from year to year. I guess I figured it would come between late January and the middle of February, and I didn't need to worry. When my mother started cleaning in a mad rush, that would be the sign it was near.

In the same way, I never wondered why we always ate fish, or why my grandparents put tangerines on top of the TV, or why the red envelopes had pictures of chubby children carrying peaches. Now I understand these symbols. Peaches would bring long life, the way noodles would, if we slurped them up without biting. Tangerines meant this was a lucky house, a house full of joy and warmth, full of orange-red fire. What more lively place to put them than on top of the TV, with its flickering pictures of beautiful people? And the fish would make us rich, because the Chinese word for "fish" sounds like the Chinese word for "plenty."

We never got rich. But we always had plenty to share.

About the Author

Janet Wong (janetwong.com) is half-Chinese and half-Korean. Born and raised in California, she remembers frantically cleaning the house each year on Lunar New Year's Eve, worrying about waking the neighbors with firecrackers, eating homemade duk gook soup on New Year's morning, and watching parades in Chinatown. She is the author of thirty books for young people, including picture books, poetry collections, and chapter books such as *Apple Pie 4th of July*, *A Suitcase of Seaweed*, and *Me and Rolly Maloo*.

About the Illustrator

Yangsook Choi (yangsookchoi.com) grew up in Korea and moved to New York to study art. She was selected as one of the most prominent new children's book artists by *Publishers Weekly*, and has written and illustrated many books for young readers. Her books have been acclaimed as "Best of the Best" by the Chicago Public Library, included on the American Library Association Notable Book list, selected by PBS Reading Rainbow, and have received the International Reading Association's Children's Book Award. Her popular picture book titles include *The Name Jar*, *Behind the Mask*, and *Gai See: What You See in Chinatown*.

Also available in Chinese and Korean Bilingual Editions